HOPSCOTCH
TWISTY TALES

Mole Versus the Enormous Turnip

by Dawn Casey

and Michael Emmerson

W
FRANKLIN WATTS
LONDON•SYDNEY

This story is based on the traditional fairy tale,
The Enormous Turnip, but with a new twist.
You can read the original story in
Hopscotch Fairy Tales. Can you make
up your own twist for the story?

Franklin Watts
First published in Great Britain in 2015 by The Watts Publishing Group

Text © Dawn Casey 2015
Illustrations © Michael Emmerson 2015

The rights of Dawn Casey to be identified as the author
and Michael Emmerson as the illustrator of this Work have been asserted
in accordance with the Copyright, Designs and Patents Act, 1988.

ISBN 978 1 4451 4299 9 (hbk)
ISBN 978 1 4451 4300 2 (pbk)
ISBN 978 1 4451 4308 8 (library ebook)

Series Editor: Melanie Palmer
Series Advisor: Catherine Glavina
Series Designer: Peter Scoulding
Cover Designer: Cathryn Gilbert

Printed in China

Franklin Watts
An imprint of
Hachette Children's Group
Part of The Watts Publishing Group
Carmelite House
50 Victoria Embankment
London EC4Y 0DZ

An Hachette UK Company
www.hachette.co.uk

www.franklinwatts.co.uk

MIX
Paper from
responsible sources
FSC® C104740
www.fsc.org

Mole lived in a snug little hole.

Above the ground, the farmer was planting seeds.

One turnip seed grew bigger
and bigger and bigger.

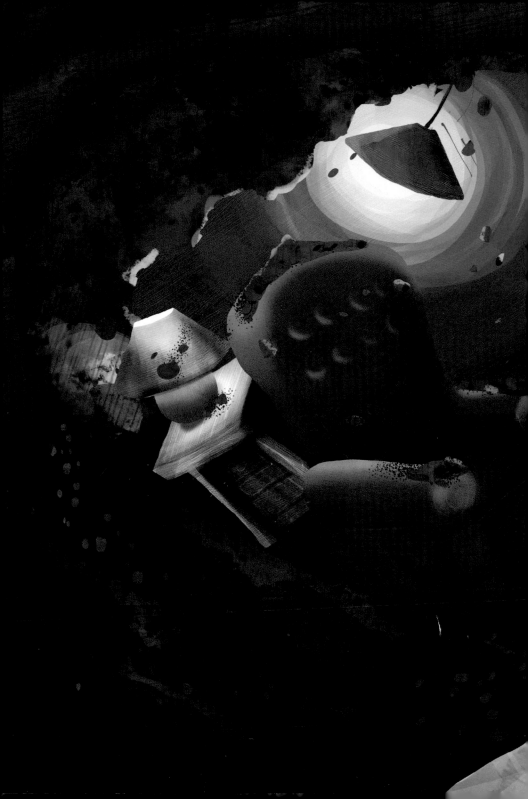

Mole's home got smaller and smaller and smaller.

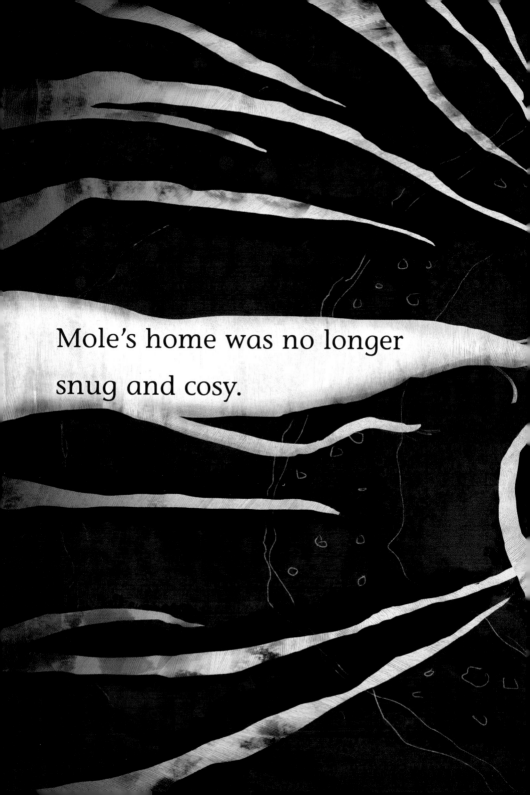

Mole's home was no longer snug and cosy.

It was squashed and squished.

"I'll sort this out," said Mole.
He rolled up his sleeves,
bent his knees and PUSHED.
But the turnip did not move.

Mole called to Badger. "Badger! Come and help me to push up this enormous turnip!"

Badger pushed Mole and Mole
pushed the enormous turnip.
But the turnip did not move.

Badger called to Rabbit. "Rabbit! Come and help us to push up this enormous turnip!"

Rabbit pushed Badger and Badger
pushed Mole and Mole pushed the
enormous turnip. But the turnip
did not move.

Rabbit called to Beetle. "Beetle! Come and help us to push up this enormous turnip!"

Beetle pushed Rabbit and
Rabbit pushed Badger and
Badger pushed Mole and Mole
pushed the enormous turnip.

POP!

Out flew

the turnip.

The farmer *was* surprised!

"Thank you," said the farmer.
"I was wondering how to get
that turnip up."

"Never mind your turnip,"
cried Mole. "Look at my home!"

"Oh!" said the farmer. "I'll help you." So the farmer worked with his spade.

And the farmer's wife worked with her needle and thread.

Badger, Rabbit and Beetle all helped Mole.

Together, everyone dug a truly
magnificent home for Mole.

Mole's new home was so big
he could invite all his friends
for a feast!

28

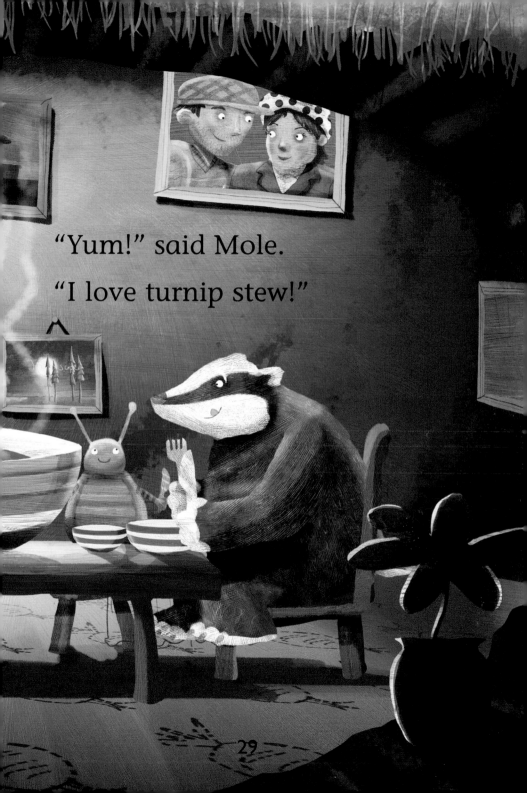

"Yum!" said Mole.

"I love turnip stew!"

Put these pictures in the correct order.
Which event do you think is most important?
Now try writing the story in your own words!

Puzzle 2

1. I need some help!

2. I have lots of seeds to plant.

3. My turnips are ready!

4. I will always help a friend.

5. My home is ruined!

6. I have big strong claws.

Choose the correct speech bubbles for each character. Can you think of any others? Turn over to find the answers.

Answers

Puzzle 1

The correct order is: 1c, 2e, 3f, 4b, 5d, 6a

Puzzle 2

Mole: 1, 5

The farmer: 2, 3

Badger: 4, 6

Look out for more Hopscotch Twisty Tales and Fairy Tales:

TWISTY TALES
The Lovely Duckling
ISBN 978 1 4451 1633 4
**Hansel and Gretel
and the Green Witch**
ISBN 978 1 4451 1634 1
The Emperor's New Kit
ISBN 978 1 4451 1635 8
**Rapunzel and the
Prince of Pop**
ISBN 978 1 4451 1636 5
**Dick Whittington
Gets on his Bike**
ISBN 978 1 4451 1637 2
**The Pied Piper and
the Wrong Song**
ISBN 978 1 4451 1638 9
**The Princess and the
Frozen Peas**
ISBN 978 1 4451 0675 5
Snow White Sees the Light
ISBN 978 1 4451 0676 2

**The Elves and the Trendy
Shoes**
ISBN 978 1 4451 0678 6
The Three Frilly Goats Fluff
ISBN 978 1 4451 0677 9
Princess Frog
ISBN 978 1 4451 0679 3

Rumpled Stilton Skin
ISBN 978 1 4451 0680 9
Jack and the Bean Pie
ISBN 978 1 4451 0182 8
**Brownilocks and the Three
Bowls of Cornflakes**
ISBN 978 1 4451 0183 5
Cinderella's Big Foot
ISBN 978 1 4451 0184 2
Little Bad Riding Hood
ISBN 978 1 4451 0185 9
**Sleeping Beauty –
100 Years Later**
ISBN 978 1 4451 0186 6

FAIRY TALES
The Three Little Pigs
ISBN 978 0 7496 7905 7
Little Red Riding Hood
ISBN 978 0 7496 7907 1
Goldilocks and the Three Bears
ISBN 978 0 7496 7903 3
Hansel and Gretel
ISBN 978 0 7496 7904 0
Rapunzel
ISBN 978 0 7496 7906 4
Rumpelstiltskin
ISBN 978 0 7496 7908 8
The Elves and the Shoemaker
ISBN 978 0 7496 8543 0
The Ugly Duckling
ISBN 978 0 7496 8544 7

Sleeping Beauty
ISBN 978 0 7496 8545 4
The Frog Prince
ISBN 978 0 7496 8546 1
**The Princess and
the Pea**
ISBN 978 0 7496 8547 8
Dick Whittington
ISBN 978 0 7496 8548 5
Cinderella
ISBN 978 0 7496 7417 5
Snow White
ISBN 978 0 7496 7418 2
**The Pied Piper
of Hamelin**
ISBN 978 0 7496 7419 9
Jack and the Beanstalk
ISBN 978 0 7496 7422 9
The Three Billy Goats Gruff
ISBN 978 0 7496 7420 5
The Emperor's New Clothes
ISBN 978 0 7496 7421 2

Enrico Empery was an ace footballer.
He was captain of Bootsville United.
He was so good that his fans
nicknamed him "The Emperor".

Enrico loved football, but he loved clothes almost as much. He wore expensive designer suits, shoes and shirts. Being rich and famous had made him a bit of a show-off.

Everyone admired "the Emperor" except for Frankie Foulo. Frankie was another star player at Bootsville United, but he knew he would never be as good as Enrico.

He watched Enrico being interviewed on television. "What a big-head," he muttered jealously. "Someone should teach him a lesson."

Bootsville United had reached the final of the cup.

"I need a new kit – something really special," said Enrico.

WELL DONE BRILLIANT!

Designers from all over the world brought all kinds of trendy kits, but none of them was special enough for the Emperor.

As he watched, Frankie thought of a trick. "I'll make Enrico look really silly," he thought, smiling.

It was the day of the big match.
Frankie took his present to Enrico.

13

"I've found you an amazing kit," Frankie said craftily.
"It's very cool because only top footballers can see it. It's invisible to all the other players."

15

Enrico ripped open the box and looked inside. He couldn't see anything! He must be a bad player. He stared sadly at the invisible kit.

He would just have to pretend that he could see it. "It's great," he fibbed. "It's brilliant!" agreed the rest of the team, who couldn't see it either.

Sass, the team mascot, arrived and heard all about the amazing kit. But the cruel trick didn't fool her. She had to put a stop to it.

19

"I bet Frankie wishes he had a kit like that," she said to Enrico. "Why don't you swap with him?"

"No way!" yelled Frankie.

But the team thought it was a great idea. So it was Frankie Foulo who went onto the pitch dressed in the Emperor's invisible new kit.

The fans whistled and hooted with laughter. Frankie blushed and hid behind a goal post until Sass found him a Bootsville United flag to wear.

Enrico Empery grinned.
"Come on, Frankie,"
he laughed. "We've got
a game to win."

27

All the crowd cheered as Frankie and the Emperor kicked the ball up into the air. The game was on.

Puzzle 1

Put these pictures in the correct order.
Which event do you think is most important?
Now try writing the story in your own words!

Puzzle 2

1. I hate show-offs.

2. I am good at spotting trouble.

3. I'm the best player!

4. I like making things fair.

5. I get jealous very easily.

6. I have lots of expensive clothes.

Choose the correct speech bubbles for each character. Can you think of any others? Turn over to find the answers.

Answers

Puzzle 1

The correct order is: 1c, 2e, 3f, 4b, 5a, 6d

Puzzle 2

The Emperor: 3, 6

Frankie Foulo: 1, 5

Sass: 2, 4

Look out for more Hopscotch Twisty Tales and Fairy Tales:

TWISTY TALES
The Lovely Duckling
ISBN 978 1 4451 1627 3*
ISBN 978 1 4451 1633 4
**Hansel and Gretel
and the Green Witch**
ISBN 978 1 4451 1628 0*
ISBN 978 1 4451 1634 1
The Emperor's New Kit
ISBN 978 1 4451 1629 7*
ISBN 978 1 4451 1635 8
**Rapunzel and the
Prince of Pop**
ISBN 978 1 4451 1630 3*
ISBN 978 1 4451 1636 5
**Dick Whittington
Gets on his Bike**
ISBN 978 1 4451 1631 0*
ISBN 978 1 4451 1637 2
**The Pied Piper and
the Wrong Song**
ISBN 978 1 4451 1632 7*
ISBN 978 1 4451 1638 9
**The Princess and the
Frozen Peas**
ISBN 978 1 4451 0675 5
Snow White Sees the Light
ISBN 978 1 4451 0676 2

**The Elves and the Trendy
Shoes**
ISBN 978 1 4451 0678 6
The Three Frilly Goats Fluff
ISBN 978 1 4451 0677 9
Princess Frog
ISBN 978 1 4451 0679 3
Rumpled Stilton Skin
ISBN 978 1 4451 0680 9
Jack and the Bean Pie
ISBN 978 1 4451 0182 8
**Brownilocks and the Three
Bowls of Cornflakes**
ISBN 978 1 4451 0183 5
Cinderella's Big Foot
ISBN 978 1 4451 0184 2
Little Bad Riding Hood
ISBN 978 1 4451 0185 9
**Sleeping Beauty –
100 Years Later**
ISBN 978 1 4451 0186 6

FAIRY TALES
The Three Little Pigs
ISBN 978 0 7496 7905 7
Little Red Riding Hood
ISBN 978 0 7496 7907 1
Goldilocks and the Three Bears
ISBN 978 0 7496 7903 3
Hansel and Gretel
ISBN 978 0 7496 7904 0

Rapunzel
ISBN 978 0 7496 7906 4
Rumpelstiltskin
ISBN 978 0 7496 7908 8
The Elves and the Shoemaker
ISBN 978 0 7496 8543 0
The Ugly Duckling
ISBN 978 0 7496 8544 7
Sleeping Beauty
ISBN 978 0 7496 8545 4
The Frog Prince
ISBN 978 0 7496 8546 1
**The Princess and
the Pea**
ISBN 978 0 7496 8547 8
Dick Whittington
ISBN 978 0 7496 8548 5
Cinderella
ISBN 978 0 7496 7417 5
Snow White
ISBN 978 0 7496 7418 2
**The Pied Piper
of Hamelin**
ISBN 978 0 7496 7419 9
Jack and the Beanstalk
ISBN 978 0 7496 7422 9
The Three Billy Goats Gruff
ISBN 978 0 7496 7420 5
The Emperor's New Clothes
ISBN 978 0 7496 7421 2

For more Hopscotch books go to:
www.franklinwatts.co.uk

*hardback